Hollie Porter's
Hat Trick
Christmas

A Revelation Cove novella

ELIZA GORDON

SGA
BOOKS

Cover and interior design by SGA Books
Nutcracker Hockey Player by Sevenstock Studio
Snowscape by Misha Kaminsky, Getty Signature
Chapter header image by Nadia Bormotova

E-book ISBN-13: 978-1-989908-55-6
Paperback ISBN-13: 978-1-989908-56-3

www.sgabooks.com | www.elizagordon.com

It wouldn't be Christmas without a little carnage . . .

"100% on-brand Hollie Porter chaos."
~ Katie Reads

Hollie Porter has her fifth Christmas with hunky hockey husband Ryan all planned out. But when a massive storm grounds her man on the mainland, Hollie must work double time to keep the Revelation Cove guests happy, fed—and rabies-free.

They say bad things come in threes, but in hockey, three goals by one player is called a hat trick. Despite weather woes, a group of masked party crashers, and a very merry strip tease gone wrong, can Hollie still score a hat trick of her own on the Big Day?

Come on up to the Cove for a hilarious holiday romp full of romance, cookies, and chaos—as if you'd expect anything less from our beloved Hollie.

For my Raft sisters,
Deb, Katie, Katrin, and LJ

Land Acknowledgment

I would like to acknowledge that I live and work on the traditional, ancestral, and unceded territory of the **Coast Salish**, **Kwikwetlem**, **Tsleil-Waututh**, **S'ólh Téméxw (Stó:lō)**, and **Qayqayt** people. I am grateful for the privilege of living in this beautiful place.

Also by Eliza Gordon

Planet Lara Series:

Welcome to Planet Lara (Book One)

Planet Lara: Tempest (Book Two)

Planet Lara: Sanctuary (Book Three)

The Revelation Cove Series:

Must Love Otters (Book One)

Hollie Porter Builds a Raft (Book Two)

Love Just Clicks (Standalone, Book Three)

Standalone novels:

Dear Dwayne, With Love

I Love You, Luke Piewalker

Books written as Jennifer Sommersby (YA):

Sleight (Book One)

Scheme (US) / *The Undoing* (Canada) (Book Two)

Fish Out of Water

Welcome back to Revelation Cove!

It's been a while. I know.

A little secret between you and me—this is my *first novella ever*. Crazy, right? I have this problem where my characters are always like *Yeah, we're in charge, not you*, and then the short story becomes a long story and forget it, now it's a novel. The author is never really in the driver's seat.

I'm excited that *this* time, I kept my eye on the prize. I decided I would write a little something as a Christmas present for my dear Rafties, a small gathering of women who cheer me on with every single word, every single rejection, every single vent session wherein I complain about life and related topics.

As a result, you, too, get a wee, adventure-filled catch-up to reacquaint yourself with our beloved Hollie Porter and Co. up at Revelation Cove.

And thank you to all the readers who have checked in on upcoming Eliza Gordon books. Two new projects are with my agent at the time of this writing, and I *do* have others on the go. I know, I'm slow. But I work full-time as an editor, so my writing time is precious. Plus, it's been one *hell* of a year with the months-long Hollywood strikes (remember that Mr. Eliza is a sculptor in the

Welcome back to Revelation Cove!

film biz. Follow his awesome TikTok: @practicalfilmmaking). I have SO many book ideas and not enough time—maybe someone has an RX for an immortality pill they'd be willing to share? I'll pay in bad jokes and sweaters knitted from cat hair.

Anyhoo, I love that we wrapped 2023 by hanging out with Hollie and Ryan. What do you think? Should I keep going?

xo,

Eliza

1

I 'll have to slip Tanner a twenty so he doesn't narc on me to his brother. If Ryan sees how many of these packages have my name on them, I'll never hear the end of it.

"Glad we brought the big boat today." Tanner winks as he pushes the wheeled blue bin down the dock. He doesn't complain about the subzero temperature or the brisk wind. He laughed when I said the sporadic scant snow looked like Zeus had scratched his scalp and then shook out the dandruff over the western British Columbia coast. He called me weird. I thanked him and boarded the Revelation Cove aquatic limousine.

"Most of these are Christmas presents. They're just addressed to me." I accept one of the bulging canvas totes as he hands it over the boat railing. As I lack the Fielding brothers' beefy biceps, the bag does not have a soft landing on the floor.

OK, so maybe I went a little nuts this year.

But can you blame me? Ryan looks hot in this particular brand of Henley I found so he needs one in every color; Miss Betty has been not so subtle in her hints about new kitchen gadgets all year (we probably should not have introduced her to the cooking influencers on Instagram), plus she has no chill when it comes to buying toys for Acorn, Chef Joseph's golden retriever who actually prefers Miss Betty to everyone else; we're doing a Secret Santa so most of the staff have sent their orders care of our P.O. box; and I do have the World's Most Incredible Niece, Elsbeth, who deserves all the latest and greatest in books, My Little Ponies, and STEM games. I'm gunning to be first on her list of thank-yous when she's accepting the Nobel, the Pulitzer, and the Fields Medal.

"One more," Tanner says, hoisting a third (fourth?) tote over the side. "Jeez, Hols, what is in this one?"

"That might be my cauldron," I say. Tanner lifts an eyebrow and wipes his bright red nose.

"This better not all be stuff for my kid."

"*Your kid* is a genius. I will do everything in my power to make sure she obliterates the competition."

"She's barely started preschool."

"Never too early to get started on that world domination, bro."

He laughs and signals that he's going to run the cart back up to the dock shed. Because Revelation Cove is nowhere near a package distribution center—and last I checked, the gray and blue Amazon trucks are not amphibious—all our online retailer orders are sent to a commercial post office in Victoria. Every few weeks, one or two among us take the three-hour boat ride south from our island, rent a ride-share vehicle from the harbor (we had an old van for such purposes, but it was stolen from the storage lot two years ago and we opted not to replace it), and empty our pickup locker where all non-food deliveries collect and wait to come home with us.

Home to *the* most beautiful place in the whole wild world. Emphasis on *wild*.

This week's load includes extra food—enough to feed half a major junior hockey team made up of seventeen- to twenty-year-old players who regularly eat double their weight. Hockey players clean out pantries like a locust swarm. I'm just glad the organization gave Ryan a per diem to feed the lads he's flying up.

Last count, at least eight of the twenty-four players will be at Revelation Cove for Christmas, along with a few members of the coaching staff and their significant others, as applicable. On top of the guests who've already arrived, we will have a very full house.

A wind buffets the side of the boat, and the water chops underfoot in our harbor moorage slip. I smile to myself as I push and pull bags and boxes into distinct piles—and maintain my balance. Over the last four and a half years of life at Rev Cove, my sea legs have grown in nicely.

Tanner unties us from the dock and then hops onto the rear deck. A shiver of excitement runs through me—after a busy morning and early afternoon of errands, pickups, and banking, we're heading north, and that means only one more sleep until the man of my dreams floats back into my life so I can unwrap my Christmas present of a different sort altogether.

2

I ate too much breakfast. I'll be burping scrambled eggs with fresh crab and onion all morning.

And I keep looking at the clock but not paying enough attention to the numbers to note the actual time. According to my clipboard of checklists, written on paper instead of one of those apps Tabby keeps bugging me to try, everything is under control.

Checklists written on paper never lie. Unless they're written in Ryan's messy script and then who knows what the hell they say. Don't tell him I said that—his handwriting sucks, but fortunately, he has other hand-focused skills that are *much* better.

Thank the gods he's coming home today. Every thought running through my mind is tainted by perversion, my dirty little mind twisting regular words into innuendo no matter the topic. It's not gone unnoticed by Tabby and Sarah, but that's only because I have zero control over my mouth when it spouts "That's what she said," à la Michael Scott of *The Office*, whenever remotely applicable. It's not my fault. I have not seen my gorgeous husband in a whole month, and I have *needs*. I can't help it if someone mentions a "poke check" while watching a hockey game and all I can think about is Ryan poke-checking me, naked. Or when they talk about excellent stick handling and I mention that Ryan has top-notch stick-handling skills.

And if all goes to plan and that float plane arrives on time, Ryan Fielding, my sex-on-a-hockey-stick demigod life partner, will earn himself a hat trick before tomorrow comes.

Heh, heh, heh, you said comes. *Get a hold of yourself.*

I glance at the clock again. "Four minutes later than the last time you looked," Miss Betty teases. She has flour on her cheek. Again. Still. She hasn't stopped baking for a week. No complaints —'tis the season of elastic-waist pants, plus the lodge's air is redolent with the heavenly aroma of gingerbread, pies, cookies, and every kind of sweet bread imaginable. My darling mother-in-law has baked so much that at least three of us have made emergency runs up the strait to Smitty's to strip his general store shelves of flour. And at least twenty pounds of yesterday's Victoria-to-Revelation-Cove cargo was baking supplies.

"He's been gone for a hundred years," I grumble, easing onto a padded stool. Miss Betty snickers and slides over a chocolate chip cookie, still melty and gooey from the oven. We are in the resort's commercial-grade kitchen, stainless steel everything, triple sinks, ferocious dishwasher that has burned me at least a dozen times, and yet, with Miss Betty here in her Christmas apron and her silver hair newly coiffed (thanks to Tabby, our resident über-stylist), this could be a scene right out of a cozy, teeth-achingly sweet Hallmark flick. (Most of which are filmed in this beautiful province, I will have you know, so yeah, we kind of have the edge on the whole Christmas vibe.)

But despite this glorious, decadent setting, my body feels like I've been caught in an on-ice melee. Between the bazillion Christmas decorations we've installed over the last three weeks and moving all those bags and boxes with Tanner yesterday and then tackling whatever was on today's to-do list (including a deep clean of our apartment since a hurricane known as Hollie lives like a single girl when (former) Concierge Ryan is on the mainland acting as (current) Hockey Coach Ryan)—yeah, I will be swallowing my Advil with a gin & 7 tonight.

5

But the lodge looks incredible, and thanks to my mad skills as Revelation Cove's director of marketing, we are booked solid through Valentine's Day. Mmm, Valentine's Day. Ryan's favorite holiday . . .

"That smile looks wicked," Tabby says, sliding onto the stool next to mine. Her cherry-red hair, twisted in a stylish updo, looks almost as festive as some of Miss Betty's baked delights.

"She's willing the clock arms to spin faster," Miss Betty adds, turning to slide another tray of cookies into the top of her double ovens.

Tabby leans against me and whispers close to my ear. "She's willing her husband's plane to fly faster so she can get a sweaty, hot dose of vitamin D for dinner."

I grin and nudge her back but not without the *Hello, no dick jokes in front of his MOM* look. Tabby sticks her tongue out at me, hoists onto the footrest of her bar stool, and steals a cookie of her own from the cooling rack.

"Speaking of vitamin D, Tabby, please remember that the young men arriving today are basically *children* and therefore unavailable for any one-on-one sessions in your salon."

"Hols, I am a grown-ass woman. The last thing I want is some tender-hearted man-child reeking of hockey gear demanding my attention." She pops the last of her cookie into her mouth. "I have better men to do." She winks and hops off her stool. "Toodles!"

And by better men, I'm pretty sure she means Nils, one of Ryan's assistant coaches. He and Tabby met at a preseason barbecue back in August, and let's just say my BFF has had an extra spring in her step these past few months. It's good. Thomas, a former member of our security team, broke her heart when he accepted a job in personal protection back east. After she fell for Thomas, she tabled her big Hollywood plans and focused on building something here. But he needed more adventure than what our quiet island had to offer. Last time we heard, he was taking bullets for dignitaries and loving every minute of it.

I'm glad to see that sparkle in Tabby's eye again. And Nils is certainly worth the sparkle.

Miss Betty hums Christmas tunes while the mixer churns with her next creation. I turn my phone over on the counter and about jump out of my skin when I see a new text.

I open it.

It's a shirtless picture of my husband.

"T-minus four hours, Porter. Comin' in hot."

That's what she said.

3

I make a final circle of the property, inside and out, because sitting in the lodge is about to drive me insane. It's effing *cold* out here but not as windy as it was in Victoria yesterday. Zeus's aforementioned dandruff floats by in half-assed flurries now and again, but nothing sticks. You'd think we'd get more snow—we are farther north, *and* this is Canada—but we're at sea level here on this rocky outcropping shoved forth from the ocean depths. If it's snowing at our lodge, you can bet the mainland is getting walloped.

This year we installed a temporary, covered outdoor "rink"—it's made of fake ice, which is probably the weirdest thing I've seen outside of one of my ex-stepmother's mescaline-fueled drum circles —but you can actually skate on it. In the long run, it was cheaper than building a proper rink with hockey-grade ice, which costs a fortune to maintain. I still have not mastered life on two blades, but at least I've provided comic relief for everyone else. And so far, knock on wood, I haven't broken my ass and required yet another emergency boat ride south for a shiny new stamp on my Island Health Authority Frequent Visitor card. (Would it be arrogant to suggest they invented that in my honor?)

Ryan hasn't seen the finished rink—or the miniature Christmas train that circles the lodge and takes riders through a forest of LED reindeer, bear, raccoon, one dog that looks a little like Acorn the dog, and yes, even a raft of otters—since we finished everything. And I have forbidden anyone from sharing photos with the boss. I want it all to be a surprise for when he flies over.

A few years ago, we halved our golf course due to environmental and financial concerns. Keeping eighteen holes of greens *green* year-round is a tremendous drain on resources, and even though we're surrounded by water, it's ocean water and we don't have the infrastructure (or space) to build a desalination plant. The islands off the coast of BC grapple with water shortages pretty much every year nowadays, which is nuts considering our location.

With a grant from a Vancouver-based eco-first company two years ago, we underwent a "rewilding" process wherein we tore up the greens (made of very dense, non-native grass) and then planted new trees, area-specific grasses, gravel and mulch walkways, and pollinator-friendly wildflowers. Miss Betty and Chef Joseph have a decent plot of garden now, Acorn has plenty of space to bury soup bones some archaeologist will uncover in a thousand years and wonder what kind of beast lived here, and guests are welcome to unwind by digging in the dirt during their downtime spent with us, weather permitting, of course.

Yeah, we took a hit with some of our golf-loving regulars since we now only have nine holes, but if I get my way, we eventually will have no holes at all.

Stop thinking about holes.

My phone buzzes in my ass pocket. A text from my sister-in-law:

"Hol, can you come up to the office?"

If Sarah's here, Elsbeth is too, and if there's anyone in the world I love as much as my dad and Ryan Fielding, it's Elsbeth.

I mean, come on, we've been friends since she squirted free of her mother's nether regions into my hands on the floor of their cabin and then held her breath for the longest minute of my entire

Eliza Gordon

life. She didn't die during my first and last foray into obstetrics, and I survived the existential crisis that came in the wake of her birth.

Our bond is sealed for eternity.

I zip my coat against the biting wind and hustle back up the trail, gravel crunching under my well-worn Timberlands.

4

"What does that mean?" I ask, balancing a very heavy Elsbeth on one hip as she attempts to braid my hair while the grown-ups talk. Bill, our facilities manager, and Tanner, Elsbeth's dad, are at the radio desk, all of us crowded into the back office. Wall-mounted computer screens monitor our security cameras, local weather patterns, local twenty-four-hour news, and communication channels for our passenger vessels, both water and air.

"It means they're grounded until this weather clears," Bill says, pointing to angry, multicolored blobs dancing across the weather screens.

"How could the weather change so fast?"

Bill shrugs. "These are the forecast models. Whichever comes true, it looks like we're getting a white Christmas."

Elsbeth whoops too close to my ear. "I love snow!"

I offer her a tight smile and kiss her still-pudgy cheek, hoping she doesn't sense my anxiety. "But tomorrow's Christmas Eve. Will they be able to fly tomorrow?"

"Environment Canada has issued a snowfall warning and travel advisories. This is a big storm. Arctic outflow is colliding with a stronger-than-expected low-pressure front moving in from the Pacific—"

"Bill, *English.*"

"We're about to get dumped on. They can't fly."

My eyes sting. "What about by boat? Tanner and I can leave now."

"I wanna go!" Elsbeth sings.

Bill's already shaking his head. "Not safe. Gusts are up measuring upward of 60 km/h along the strait and running south. And with the freezing level at zero, you'll be in white-out conditions on the water."

The room gets very quiet, other than the low buzz of radio chatter from the two-way.

A tiny, slightly sticky hand grips my chin and turns my head. "Unca will be here for Christmas, Hollie Cat." I love how she adopted my dad's pet name for me. "I asked Santa."

I squeeze Elsbeth in a tight hug and hope that Santa listens to this kid who's in the top 1 percent of the Nice List.

5

After what feels like a million tries, Ryan finally picks up. "Sorry, babe. It's a mess over here. Trying to figure out who's going where since some of guys, their billet families have already left town."

"Are you back at the apartment?" With the hockey club's help, Ryan rented a place near the Langley arena for him to live during the season. Even though I miss him desperately when he's off island, it's nice to have a landing pad on the Lower Mainland when I need to take meetings, do supply runs, or have nekked alone time with the world's hottest hockey coach.

"Yeah. I've got five kids with me. Nils has three at his place. The roads are chaos."

"The storm hasn't even hit yet."

"You guys don't have snow?"

"No."

"It's coming down pretty good here," he says. "But you know how Vancouverites are in the winter."

"Laughingstock of Canada, I know." I want to be lighthearted and positive that Christmas isn't a total wash, but at this point . . . "Do you have enough food to feed all the guys?"

"I'll send them down the block to the store. It'll give 'em a chance to burn off some of this energy."

"Do we even have enough blankets for everyone?"

"We'll figure it out," he says. "I can hear the worry in your voice, Hol. I promise I will get home as soon as I can."

"Yeah, no, I know. It's just . . . it's Christmas. I was looking forward to seeing you."

"Me too. But as soon as we're given the all-clear, we're out of here. Promise."

"'K . . ." *Don't be a baby and cry about this. Suck it up. Safety first.* "Elsbeth said she's asked Santa to bring Unca home for Christmas."

"Well, if anyone can get through to that old jolly bastard, it's Els."

We talk about lodge business for a few minutes, how most of our holiday guests have already arrived and checked in, so we have an almost full house. The few cancelations we've received have been tentative only, as in if the storm disappoints the glee-riddled meteorologists and the passenger shuttle is allowed to run again by Boxing Day, the guests would still love to come up and spend a few days between then and New Year's.

I'm midsentence when the back office goes dark. "Shit."

"What?"

"The power just went out."

Ryan is quiet for a beat. "I'll let you go. Call me with updates. I love you."

"Me too," I say, disconnecting. For the first time, I realize that ache in my chest isn't just because I miss my husband—it's because I'm pissed off that he's not here to deal with this, that he's hours of travel away from *his* lodge and family, that I am not in Portland with my dad this year since Ryan and his business partners wanted to do something "big and special" for Christmas, so I've worked tirelessly over the last year putting everything together, creating dream packages for guests, running very successful ads campaigns, and pulling off the impossible with Bill and Tanner to organize the fake-ice rink and the ride-on train and the stupid light-up creatures that cost a fortune and took forever to arrive.

For the first time since Ryan Fielding and I crossed paths four and a half years ago, I want to punch *his* lights out.

6

I slouch in the comfy wheeled chair, the back office dim save for the single battery-powered LED camp lamp and the glow of only two of the eight computer screens. A beefy biomass generator hums along the western exterior of the building, delivering enough juice for the bare necessities. Weather and security feeds, refrigerators, the walk-in freezer, one heat pump to keep the main dining room and ballroom warm, interior safety lights now that the sun has gone to bed, as well as the electric fireplace inserts in the guest rooms. On the monitor tracking the incoming storm, that menacing red clot grows closer with every Doppler rotation, and I stare at it as if I possess some magical telepathic ability to change the will of the weather gods.

You will turn to rain. You will stop blowing boats around for your perverse amusement. You will bring Hollie's hot hubby home. Weather gods, hear my plea.

The door bursts open, startling me from my tired trance, and Tabby stands with hands on her shapely hips. "Everyone's waiting in the ballroom."

"For what?"

"It was your idea to put on a Christmas pageant."

"It's a talent show."

"Whatever it is, it's time to pay the piper."

"What does that even mean?" I whine as she pulls me out of the chair.

"It means if you don't get in there and start bossing people around, they're gonna start drinking."

"We have guests to take care of. I can't have the whole staff drunk."

"Then move your butt."

"I should've taken Smitty up on that offer for a living nativity."

"Yes, because nothing says Merry Christmas like three blind sheep, an earless donkey, and a gnarly alpaca dressed as a camel."

"Yeah, what happened to the donkey's ears?"

She stomps her foot.

"*Fine.*" I stop resisting and allow her to drag me toward the ballroom just off the main lobby and down the hall. Before the door is even open, we are blasted with the discordant sounds of a not-great cover band warming up.

"You should not have told the maintenance crew they sound good when they make those noises," I say.

"Those noises are a guitar, drums, and bass."

"And the song they're murdering? We should plan a funeral."

We pause outside the doors. "You're right. Eddie Van Halen is rolling in his grave." Tabby crosses herself, as if she weren't the *least* Catholic person I know. "We are sorry for what they're doing to your music, Mr. Van Halen. Amen."

"Amen," I echo.

She opens the door and the "music" hits me smack in the face. "How do they have power for the amp?" I ask.

"Brad has a battery pack," Tabby yells, pointing at the raised platform that serves as the ballroom's stage. Sure enough, our maintenance lead is scratching his pick across the strings of his guitar with such vigor, I will have workers' comp claims for hearing loss within the hour.

"Maybe this was a bad idea," I yell back to compete with the din.

"You think?" Tabby loops her arm through mine and drags me

to the stage, drawing a finger across her neck in the universal sign to the "musicians" to STFU. Even with the battery-powered camp lamps on every other circular banquet table and the auxiliary emergency lights burning a muted yellow from soffits around the room's edge, it's a little creepy in here. And once Brad stops molesting his poor guitar, the wind's ferocity becomes more obvious, howling like it's interested in booking a spa day.

I step onto the small stage, heart skipping every third beat from my thinly stretched nerves. I'm not great with public oratory. And every time I'm in this room, I think of my first time at Revelation Cove when I partook of my patio hot tub, inadvertently locked myself out of my room, stark naked, and ended up in the lobby where Concierge Ryan took great joy in offering me a woefully tiny dishtowel. I then happened upon a banquet in progress wherein I provided comic relief for a room full of horny businessmen before yanking free a tablecloth to stand in for evening wear. Heat prickles the back of my neck revisiting that fun night.

"Hey, everyone." Thirty or so faces smile, smirk, or stare back at me. Not everyone is Team Hollie. That's OK. As long as they're Team Get My Job Done, that's all I care about. (It's taken three long years of therapy via Zoom to be able to say that and *almost* believe that I don't need everyone to like me.) "So, Ryan and his guys are stuck in Vancouver until the storm lets up. Bill and Tanner are keeping an eye on the weather reports, and thanks very much to our fix-it crew for getting the generator up and going so fast."

Brad bows to whoops and hollers, his right arm draped along the top of his electric guitar. Behind him, Lawry does a one-two tap on his middle drum. A chuckle murmurs through the crowd.

"Until the power is restored, we will run on a minimal operations schedule. The guest-room fireplace inserts will work as long as we have generator fuel, but if we can coax folks to gather in the main dining area or in here to conserve resources, we can then offer free drinks or coffee and tea and whatever holiday delights Miss Betty has been baking up for us—" Another round of hoots and applause interrupts me. *Everyone* here is on Team Betty, as it should be. She waves her appreciation from her padded banquet chair, her flour-splattered apron still tied around her front. Acorn, yet another Christmas-print bandana tied around his golden neck, barks his approval.

"Chef assures me we have plenty of food on hand, including fruit and veg that can be prepped and served without need to turn on the ovens. I don't think this storm should last more than twenty-four hours. This *is* the Pacific Northwest, am I right?" I smile, hoping to see it reflected at me.

Instead, another gust slams into the building, the wood and concrete and stonework structure groaning against the blow. "Um, yeah, so I think we should postpone or even cancel the talent show to save——"

The rest of my sentence is buried under an avalanche of disagreement.

Tabby hops up onto the stage next to me and whistles between her fingers. Damn, I wish I could do that. "Listen up, dorks. Let her finish."

The crowd quiets again. I need to get this out quickly—we only have five staffers minding things while the rest of us are in this superfluous meeting. "We don't know what the next twenty-four hours will bring, how soon the power will come back, how long this storm plans on hanging around, how much snow——"

"All the more reason to do the show!" someone chirps.

"Yeah, we can entertain the guests and keep their minds off everything else. It will be like summer camp, except it's winter," someone else adds.

Tabby turns to me, eyebrows raised in question. "That's not a terrible idea," she murmurs. The room chatter increases again, everyone expressing opinions about why the show must go on.

"I'm not trying to be a party pooper," I say, raising my hand in the hopes they will shut up. Tabby tucks her fingers into her lips, threatening her deafening whistle again. They shush, although the wind has now added a new ingredient to its smacking against the double-paned, east-facing windows: snow.

Like, a *lot* of white. A proper blizzard.

"Um, so my biggest concern here is the comfort of our guests. We need to ration our generator power so we don't end up running out of the fuel that feeds it."

Brad raises his hand, but the look on his face tightens my throat. "Um, about that . . ."

7

Since I primarily work in marketing these days (and still offer my wildlife education tours to our youngest guests), I don't have my finger on the pulse of everything in the operations department. That's a Bill and Brad and Tanner thing and a Ryan thing when he's here. This is not a Hollie thing.

Which is why Brad telling me in front of everyone that we have enough biomass fuel for *maybe* two days, tops, is not awesome. "We were supposed to get another fuel delivery for the genis two weeks ago, but our guy had a disruption in receiving the stuff we use from his supplier. These biomass generators are getting really popular."

I know nothing about biomass generators, other than they're better for the environment. I didn't think I would ever need to know anything about biomass generators because *it's not my job to know about biomass generators*. I know how to create lookalike audiences and interpret analytics and target my demographic on ads platforms and I know a thing or two about *Enhydra lutris* and *Orcinus orca* and how to stop a gaping wound from bleeding out, none of which requires a degree in biomass generators.

"Well, now we definitely need to cancel the talent show. We

cannot waste an ounce of electricity on anything not considered a priority."

Bill, seated at a front table, raises his hand. "We have about five cords of wood dried and stacked for use in the fireplace in the dining room. Let's keep it stoked so we can conserve geni power by not heating that huge space."

"Great idea. Thank you. Anyone else?" I scan the room, looking for more suggestions, but I receive only dour, disappointed faces. "We can totally reschedule the talent show once we know our guests won't freeze to death. Also, if you haven't picked up the gift you ordered for the Secret Santa, pop by the break room and have a look in the totes. There are still quite a few unclaimed packages, and everything needs to be wrapped and labeled for tomorrow's gift exchange. OK, thanks. Send any relevant updates or concerns via the group chat."

The head housekeeper lifts her phone above her head. "The Wi-Fi is out. And I only have, like, one bar from the cell tower."

Tabby and I exchange looks. *Shit.* I forgot about Wi-Fi. Few years back, the country's biggest wireless provided installed a cell tower a few miles from here, camouflaged in the vast forest and meant to improve communications for boats, ferries, planes, and local residents, but it's temperamental during inclement weather, despite us paying a king's ransom in monthly fees.

Miss Betty stands and faces the group. "Long before we had all these fancy devices, we used a message board and *wrote* down our dispatches to one another. I'll wheel it out of storage and set it up behind the concierge desk so we can post notes and updates and that sort of thing to keep everything moving smoothly."

Great idea, except I don't think Miss Betty realizes they stopped teaching handwriting in school years ago. Good luck interpreting the chicken scratch of our team members.

"OK, let's pause the show plans for now, focus on our guests, and man those battle stations!" I try to sound chipper and not freaked out. Tabby hides a smirk behind her hand.

Amid grumbles and commentary I can't quite hear, the staff push in chairs and collect whatever props they brought along for today's rehearsal. Brad lifts his guitar over his head and shuffles toward his amp, a shriek of feedback echoing through the room. I follow as he kneels to replace his instrument in its case. Bill and Tanner clomp onto the stage behind me.

"So, this seems kinda bad, right?" I ask. The three men look at one another, though Tanner speaks first.

"Nah. We've seen worse. We'll be fine."

It's almost as if Fate was waiting for someone to say that out loud.

Because all the lights powered by the generator blink us into near black.

8

Our big plans for the generator to keep the guest rooms warm —ha ha ha ha ha—yeah, no. Bill and his team bundle up and head out to diagnose whatever the hell is wrong with the super fancy, *very* expensive biomass geni while Brad and his guys trudge to the maintenance shed to retrieve the two smaller gas generators we retired but hung on to for this very reason.

We have to keep the fridges and walk-in working, no matter what. The one hundred and twenty-odd people currently under our roof will likely not appreciate crackers and granola bars and warm beer for Christmas dinner, plus losing thousands of dollars' worth of food was not on this week's handwritten to-do list. I know because I double-checked my clipboard and *nope*, it wasn't there.

The lobby fills with guests who we direct into the main dining room where a huge fire blazes in the hearth. We're lucky in that the people staying with us aren't high-maintenance whiners—at least not yet. Let's see what happens if the guys can't get at least minimum power flowing again. Not sure how patient everyone will be about sleeping on the dining room floor just to keep warm.

The most popular question after "Does BC Hydro service this island?" is "Do you have any way for us to charge our phones?"—a question I have also pondered in the last hour or so after noticing the dwindling battery icon on my own device. I have a pocket charger bank thingie that Ryan bought me last year as a stopgap as I am constantly dancing on the brink.

Do I know where that charger is? No. Will it be charged even if I do find it? Absolutely not.

Whereas before I was worried about Wi-Fi, now I realize that Wi-Fi doesn't matter if your phone is dead.

Wait—Brad has the battery pack he was using to power his guitar. We can use that!

Except Brad has disappeared, likely to throw on his winter gear so he can head into the whiteout to deal with the generators.

An actual whiteout. HOW did that hit so fast?

I check my phone again. Battery's at 16%. It'll be fine. Besides, the guys will have us up and running in no time. Right?

"Hollie," Miss Betty calls, waving to me from behind the concierge desk. She's talking to Cam, a strapping young lad who took Ryan's spot as concierge as she fiddles with a giant key ring to open the storage closet. While we keep life jackets and safety equipment for water sports within, I don't think we have toboggans or sleds. Seems a little dangerous since sliding down a snowy mound will likely deposit a person into the frigid waters of the Salish Sea.

"What can I do for you?" I ask, right as she finds the correct key and swings open the door.

And is met with angry chitters and hisses from a *very* large momma raccoon standing on her hind legs, claws readied for battle.

9

"How did they even get in there?" Miss Betty asks, her hand flattened over her heart as she leans against the hastily closed door. Acorn's unceasing bark echoes in my skull.

"I saw at least three babies," I say, kneeling to calm the dog.

"I counted four," Cam adds.

"OK. This is fine. They're just cold and scared. They must've wandered in when the doors were propped open or something." I close my eyes and push my fingers against my eyelids, hard enough that a constellation bursts in my blackened vision.

"How did they get past Acorn? And how will we get them out of there without raising a ruckus?" Miss Betty asks. The tone of her voice unsettles me—Miss Betty is usually a pillar of strength, the Every Mom who has all the answers no matter the situation. Sprained an ankle due to poor choices in footwear? Here's some ice. Broken fingers after an attack from a protective daddy crow? Here's a couple aspirin. Delivering a baby on the floor of a nearby cabin? Grab some towels and hot water. Miss Betty just *knows* stuff. She says it's a mom thing.

The only thing my mom knows is how to disappear and break

laws and crash weddings. Although I hear in her new digs, she's learning how to make license plates.

Tanner blows through the front doors like the Abominable Snowman. In his right hand, the scoopy part of a snow shovel; in his left, the shovel's broken-off wooden handle. "Snow's heavier than it looks," he announces, stamps his frosted boots on the huge industrial door mat, and freezes. "What's wrong?" He looks first to me, then Cam, then his mom and Acorn. "You look like you've seen a ghost." He drops the dearly departed shovel and removes his gloves. Tanner doesn't have Ryan's bulk, but they have the same walk, the same mannerisms when worried.

Seeing his face as he looks at his mom zaps me with a fresh jolt of melancholy—and frustration—that Ryan isn't here.

"A family of raccoons has taken up residence in the storage closet," Miss Betty offers. Tanner pauses to pat the dog on the head and accept obligatory slobbery licks to his sweaty hand and then wraps an arm around his mom's shoulders.

"Is that all? You look a lot more worried than some misdirected trash pandas."

Miss Betty looks up at her son. "I hid everyone's Christmas presents in there. And I still need to wrap everything."

Above us, the lights flicker back to life, the massive lobby Christmas tree blinking awake in all her twinkly glory. A round of cheers echoes through the building.

"OK, Mom, don't worry about the raccoons. We have power!" Tanner says, thrusting a fist skyward as if inviting his personal lightning bolt to high-five him. I wish he wouldn't tempt the gods, especially after I just made so many demands of them about the weather.

"Miss Betty," I say, stepping beside her, "the communication board can wait. We probably won't even need it. If we have power, we have internet. We can message the guests in the lodge group chat with whatever we need to announce. Everything's gonna work out."

She nods, but Tanner's right. She looks more worried than normal.

Then again, Christmas Eve is in a few hours, we have raccoons

27

Eliza Gordon

in the storage room, Ryan is AWOL, and we are under fearsome attack by Mother Nature's tempestuous middle daughter, Frosty McBitchface.

"You still have that stash of Bailey's in the back office?" I ask her. "Come on. Let's go see if we can find it."

10

With the power partially restored, the wall of monitors is again lit up like our own personal Times Square. Feed from the regional news station shows intrepid reporters standing like bent trees on darkened street corners, clutching their mics close while broadcasting about the ferocious winds and white-out conditions. A chyron rolls across the bottom of the screen that reads "Transport Canada is asking motorists to stay home unless it's an emergency. Road conditions are treacherous."

My heart plops into my gut to feel sorry for itself.

With Miss Betty nestled into one of her floral-print wingback chairs that look like they belong in an English teahouse, a steaming cup of Bailey's and coffee in her grip, *Downton Abbey* on one of the monitors, and Acorn curled at her feet snoring away, I check my phone. Battery is at 12%. But we have power, so I can charge it. Duh!

When I plug it in, low power mode disengages, and my notifications light up on the group chat we use for guest communication. Since I'm the one who lured so many of our current residents to Revelation Cove with the promise of a magical

Christmas getaway, my DMs have way more messages than the other channels:

Hi Hollie, any idea when the power will be back?

I'm in room 28 and the fireplace insert isn't working. It's freezing. Can you please send someone over?

Is dinner still on for tonight? We have to EAT something. A little communication would be great.

The kids were really hoping to go on your Christmas train. When will that be an option?

Hullo? I keep calling the front desk to have champagne sent to our room but no one's answering. Does anyone work here?

Plus another twenty or so messages asking about how to charge their devices if the power doesn't come back on, two asking if they will be given a discount or refund due to the inconveniences, and—not even kidding—the couple in one of our suites asking if we can fly them back to Vancouver because "you didn't tell us there would be a blizzard."

That thing I said about no high-maintenance guests?

I lied.

I'd rather check in an entire gaze of raccoons.

11

Chef and his small but talented team whip together a sumptuous late dinner, served in the dining room for everyone to partake of. A few whines are uttered about the limited menu, but thankfully, the stink-eye from surrounding tables when seen harassing a member of the waitstaff amid these insane circumstances keeps everything to a dull roar. People are braver in the comfort of their rooms—they can send snarky messages without having to look me in the eye. Here in the public forum, bitching and moaning about this unexpected weather tantrum earns the bitcher and moaner an unfriendly eyebrow hike from those within hearing range.

Good.

Our forward-thinking Chef preps breakfast and lunch for tomorrow while we have electricity, his kitchen a well-oiled machine. Christmas Eve dinner is supposed to be a massive charcuterie spread—much of it already prepared and resting in the walk-in—so we should be able to feed people through tomorrow, knock on wood. When I asked him about Christmas dinner, touted in my Christmas package sales pitch as "the biggest feast of Pacific Northwest delights this side of the Rockies," Chef handed me a steaming twice-baked potato on a cake plate and told me to get out of his kitchen.

I guess that's a wait-and-see, then?

With full bellies and beer-soaked brains, our guests return to their quarters with instructions to remain inside the lodge until the storm settles. Bill and Brad and Tanner found the reason for the biomass generator's hiccup—wires chewed clean through—but that doesn't eliminate the problem of us running out of fuel by the twenty-sixth. And Bill talked to his guy at BC Hydro who said it could be up to a week before they get to us.

A week. *A week?*

This is not ideal. We will have to empty the lodge if we can't get power back on before the generators run dry.

Tanner will know what to do.

He and Sarah and Elsbeth live in a cabin a few miles south on another island, but obvs they're camped out here with us until further notice. Miss Betty's suite has enough room to accommodate, and there's little she loves more than having Elsbeth as a roommate. And Els, drunk on sugar when Sarah scooped her from the posse of lodge kids playing in the main dining room, shrieked her goodbyes to her new friends from her perch over her mother's shoulder as they traipsed down the main hallway. One would think she was about to board a spacecraft for exploration of distant galaxies, never to be seen again. "Goodbye, my friends! I love you! I will miss you!"

Tanner vows to get his little family settled and then return so we can see about reintroducing Momma Raccoon to her natural environs—except the snow is still sheeting down, the wind still yelling at our doors and windows. I counter that we offer the raccoons a free night's lodging right where they are, safe and warm, and that Tanner go to bed and let me handle things for a while. He is slow to agree, but judging by his wind-burned cheeks and bright red nose that won't stop running, I'd guess he's too exhausted to risk any further threats to his well-being this evening.

I absolutely can appreciate that.

And in all honesty, I'll take a family of trapped raccoons over an agitated cougar (or demon goat) any day.

"Don't tell Elsbeth about the kits. She'll want to make friends with them," he says, scrubbing a hand through his hat hair.

"They are pretty damn cute."

"Have you not learned your lesson?" He snorts. "See you in four hours." Tanner mock salutes me and disappears down the hall toward his mom's suite. We've decided to monitor the front desk in shifts to give everyone a chance to rest. Though the lodge typically has a night agent, Hannah, she's in Ontario visiting family until the second week of January. And since I can't sleep because I'm worried about Ryan and Christmas and electricity and raccoons, I volunteered for the first shift.

Upon checking the lodge messages, it appears everyone has been placated with complimentary bottles of whatever they wanted, and the most urgent demands have been met. Again, it's always funny to see how aggressive people can be from behind a keyboard but then in person, they're like, *Oh, no, don't worry about it.* Another thing I've noticed in my almost five years in Canada? Canadians tend to back down when confronted. Some will bluster and gripe until you stand up to them or give them lip back, and then the passive aggression clicks on: *Now don't get so angry, I didn't mean to upset you.*

I've only ever had one woman clap back at me—in a Canadian Tire parking lot when she wouldn't get out of the crosswalk, so I squealed my tires at her. She startled so hard, she dropped her cigarette and came after me where I parked. It felt good to be American again for a few minutes of heated parking-lot screeching.

And then when we passed each other in the housewares aisle inside the store, you'd never know anything happened. Well, except for the matching middle fingers we raised like flags at each other. Ryan was so embarrassed, he sent me to the car to wait for him to finish his shopping.

Speaking of Ryan, I should call him. Check in. What time is it?

My phone sits in the charging dock at the front counter, and I am SO thankful to see that red battery icon replaced with its healthier green comrade. It's quiet down here now with only an hour left before it's officially Christmas Eve, everyone else snug in their beds. The LED Christmas tree lights are on a dimmer, giving off a muted reflection against the howling night just outside the huge west-facing wall of double-paned windows. Since we're on generator power, any unneeded lights and electronics are off, the lobby and entry area cast in eerie shadow. With so much silence, I can hear Momma Raccoon chittering to her babies in the storage closet. Probably telling them to go to sleep or Santa won't come tomorrow night. Maybe I should go to the kitchen and get them something—

My phone buzzes with a call, and I about jump out of my skin.

"Babe!" I answer.

"Hey, Porter … you OK up there? Everyone safe?"

"Yeah, the guys got the geni back up and running. Looks like something chewed through a few wires. Oh, and we have raccoons living in the storage closet, but other than that . . ."

He snickers. I hear a rousing game of something in the background. "Hold on a sec—" The sound fades and a door clicks closed. "I forgot how much energy teenage boys have, especially when they can't burn it off on the ice."

"You guys are all right, though?"

"We're fine. They're eating everything in sight, Skip the Dishes has been here four times, and they're playing video games. Aggressively. At least three neighbors have knocked on the door to complain about the noise."

Despite this, it's quiet for a beat. "I miss you, Ryan Fielding."

"What are you wearing?"

I hear the smile in his voice. "Revelation Cove khaki."

"Mmmm, I love it when you talk dirty."

"I'm minding the front desk. We're taking shifts."

"Can't people just chill out long enough for you guys to get some sleep?"

"You'd think." I sigh. "I wish you were here."

"I know. I will try everything in my power to get there for Christmas Day. This storm can't last forever."

"Feels like it."

"Aww, someone sounds like they have a case of the sads."

"More like a case of *where is my hot husband because he's not in my panties*."

"Ohhhh . . . more of that, please."

"Seriously, Ryan. This is dumb. I've been counting down the minutes until you were gonna be home."

"I know. I have too, babe. The guys have been teasing me about being an asshole lately, saying they can't wait for me to reunite with my woman so I can get my happy back."

I stand and do a quick scan of the foyer and attached hallways to make sure no one is on their way to complain about the towels not being soft enough or that the moon is hidden by the storm clouds. All clear, so I set the shiny service bell on the counter, open the door to the back office, and tiptoe in. No one else is here, but I'm afraid to make too much noise. Might disturb the raccoons.

"Call me back on FaceTime," I say. "Give me two minutes to set up my laptop."

"I like the sound of that."

"And when you call, I want you naked," I demand.

"I have an apartment full of teenage horndogs."

"So go into the bathroom and lock the door." He starts to protest but I cut him off. "If you don't do as I say, you'll regret it when you finally do reunite with your woman."

"Yes, ma'am. Two minutes. Naked. In the bathroom."

My cheeks ache with a wicked grin. It's not the first time we've had cyber marital relations, and it's nothing like the real thing, but if seeing my husband's shredded form sans clothing, his various parts happy to see me, even from a distance . . . I'll take whatever I can get on this cold winter's night.

I grab my laptop from my backpack, open it on the painted antique desk, then lean over to flip the lock. We don't have security cameras back here and this small room has no windows and only the single door, so I'm safe from intrusion. With all but two monitors dark—the weather one and the main security feed—I click off the second lamp so I'm lit only by the one behind my computer on the desk. I turn on the laptop's camera to check my position and lighting, my heart racing as the two minutes tick away.

Ryan's profile picture—him in full hockey regalia, an action shot from when he was playing with the Canucks—lights up my screen. I click on it, pleased to see he followed my instructions.

"You're still clothed," he growls.

"I am. I thought you might want to watch that part."

"You thought correctly."

I click play on my Music app. Chris Isaak's "Wicked Game" starts, and Ryan laughs on the other end of our connection. "Fuck me, Ry, I have missed that smile." My eyes sting. Then Chris's sultry voice floats from the speakers and I remember my mandate. Slowly, I untuck my forest-green Revelation Cove shirt from my beige uniform cargos, lifting it just enough to show my belly button, gyrating as I unhook my black leather belt and pull it from the loops, folding it in half and slapping it against my palm before dropping it to the floor. Slowly, I lift the shirt above my head and whip it around once before tossing it over my shoulder.

Ryan laughs again, but he has that look on his face he gets right before he heats up. Pupils dilating, the way he bites his lower lip, runs a hand through his dark brown curls. I love that look. I *live* for that look.

I play with the top button of my pants, unbutton, and turn a slow spin to make sure he has a clear picture of my backside.

"Is that a new bra?" His voice is husky.

I face front and lean close so he gets a better look at the lace. I'm not busty, but this bra does my existing boobs a real favor. "Consider it an early Christmas present."

"Tell me it's a matching set," he whispers. I step back and slide my pants down over my hips. "Jesus, Hols . . ."

It is indeed a matching set.

As Chris Isaak croons about not wanting to fall in love, I turn away from the camera again, reaching behind me to unfasten the lacy bra—*sproing!*—a peek over my shoulder, throw in a little ass wiggle. My bra is only held to my body by my right hand, and I slowly turn to face the camera again, letting one cup drop to reveal some boob. Ryan's answering smile is molten, and from the slight shimmy of the camera on his end, I know he's handling a job I usually enjoy.

"Naked," he demands. Chris Isaak fades out but restarts—I knew this might take longer than the song's duration—and I don't miss a beat, doing my best to look sexy. Hand lifted, my bra tumbles to the floor, and I slide a finger along the waistband of my lace panties, daring to push one side down to give my husband a glimpse of his personal playground.

His smile has grown serious, his breaths shortening.

I ease my hand under the left side of my panties and slide them down, bending so he gets a full view of my top half while I step out of my underwear, pluck them from the floor, and give them a playful twirl above my head. No idea where they land once they fling free.

Ryan and I have done this before, and while my shyness about undressing on camera has not completely disappeared, we do have a line. Nothing too explicit, no spread-eagle chach shots. Who knows who might be hacked in and watching from some dank basement in Calgary.

I gyrate and spin and wiggle through another minute or two, touching parts unknown off-camera since, after nearly five years together, I know what Ryan likes—

Ding.

I startle but resume my rhythm so my handsome partner doesn't detect a thing.

"*What a wicked thing to do … to make me dream of you …*"

Ding ding.

Shit. That's the front desk bell. *Keep dancing.*

"Damn, Hols, you are so beautiful …"

Ryan is getting closer, so although the sensuous bubble on this side has popped, I want him to—

Ding ding ding ding ding ding ding.

Fuck!

Whoever is molesting the bell will wake the raccoons, if not the entire lodge. If Ryan doesn't speed things up, who knows how long this dinging will go on. I ease into another slow hip-rolling rotation to surreptitiously turn away from the camera, scanning for my far-flung garments—

Whoever is at the front desk is now dinging *and* hooting. "Hello? Is anyone back there?"

Come on, Ryan.

Ding ding ding ding ding is followed by a *knock knock KNOCK.*

Ryan pauses, face flushed but not quite the flush I was going for. "Hollie, is someone in the background?"

"A guest is banging on the door. I am so sorry—hang on. I need to find my underwear—"

The door to the tiny back office opens, light from out front flooding into my darkened love den. I shriek and attempt to cover myself with my hands. "I'll be right with you!" I yell at the boomer-aged dude gawking at me, his hand still on the doorknob.

"Oh! Sorry! We just need—"

"OUT!" I yell.

He splutters and backs away from the door, though he leaves it open. I bound after him and slam it closed.

"Did you not lock it?" Ryan barks.

"Of course I locked it!" I scurry around to collect my clothes, throwing my arms through my bra, shirt over my head. "Where are my fucking panties?" I search in the dimly lit space and in my haste to click on another lamp, I knock it over and the bulb smacks, breaks, and blinks out. "Shit!"

"Damn, Hols, slow down and don't cut yourself. Get dressed first and deal with the broken glass after."

"I can't find my underwear," I spit. Fuck it. I pull on my cargo pants, commando, and gather my hair into a ponytail at my nape. "I'm sorry. I'll call you back."

Ryan has now stood and turned on the shower. "Go deal with your intruder. I will call you at first light with an update."

"Shit, this whole thing really sucks, Ryan. FaceTime sex once every two weeks is not conducive to a happy marriage."

Ryan's expression sours—I know that look. Even though we both agreed to this living arrangement while he's coaching, it doesn't mean I haven't bitched about it on more than one occasion.

I can't help it. I miss him. He's my best friend. I miss everything about him, and this longing only intensifies knowing he won't be home for Christmas.

"I'm sorry, Hols. I'll call you in a few hours. Love you." He hangs up.

"Bloody hell . . ." I mumble, throwing open the back-office door.

The guest at the front desk better be here to report a goddamn earthquake or volcanic eruption because his interruption of my happy funtime with my stud lover boy has resulted in some serious seismic fallout.

12

"He walked in on you?" Tabitha asks, voice lowered as she hunches over her cup of Matcha.

"Stark-ass naked."

"Did he see anything?"

"Pretty sure he saw everything." I sip my black coffee, not because I love the taste of motor oil after four hours of not-great sleep but because I'm too effing tired to walk back to the kitchen and find sugar and creamer.

"And Ryan was on FaceTime?"

"Yes." I cringe.

"Was he—"

"Stop." I shake my head at my friend. Tabby and I are close, yeah, but I don't have to share every morsel with her. *No, Tabitha, my husband was not able to reach fruition of his one-handed carnal adventure because Ivan Interrupter from room 34 decided he needed more freaking bath towels.*

We're sitting in the almost empty ballroom at a table nearest a roaring wood-burning fireplace that hardly ever gets used. It's Christmas Eve, the main dining room across the lobby is packed with guests who've decided they do indeed still like us, and yes, the worst of the storm has passed. That's not to say we're out of the woods yet. We're still running on generators, and BC Hydro has not moved up the estimation of when they will restore us. While the blizzard has stopped, the wind picked up where its flaked sibling left off, hitting about 35 knots along the coast, which means vessels of the air and water variety are still not cleared to operate.

I've already done a walkabout this morning with Bill and Tanner. We have almost two feet of snow and the temps are subzero, the wind chill bitingly colder. The cloud cover will break open now and again to reveal stunning hints of blue, but then more threatening gray and white pillows blow in, as if to say, *Nope, you've looked your fill of the turquoise hope, back to despair you go.*

I think if Ryan were here and not stuck in Langley, I would be thrilled about being snowed in.

But he's not, and it's too cold and brisk for Elsbeth to make a snowman or for the other lodge kids to skate on our stupid fake-ice rink or for Tanner to dress in his conductor's hat and drive guests around in circles on that ridiculous train.

"OK, that's it," Tabby says, slapping her hand on the table. I jump in my seat, splashing coffee onto my pants. "You're being a total Grinch, that Bah Humbug guy—what was his name? Cratchit?"

"No, Bob Cratchit is the good guy. He has the sick kid with the old-fashioned crutch—Jimmy. No, Timmy."

"What's the bad guy's name? The dude who bitches about Christmas so all the ghosts come and chew him out."

A couple seconds pass while we dig through memory banks.

"Ebeneezer!" / "Scrooge McDuck!" we announce in unison.

"His first name is Ebeneezer," I clarify.

"Whatever. Scrooge. You're being a lame-ass Scrooge. Yeah, your man isn't here to tickle your fancy bits, but there are a ton of other people who would be really happy about some Christmas entertainment."

I know where this is going. I shake my head. "We can't. Generators will run out of juice."

"Bullshit. The big expensive one, maybe, but we have enough

gas to keep the other two going to get us through the First Annual Revelation Cove Christmas Pageant Extravaganza!"

I do not like where this is going. I don't want to be happy. I want to pout and feel sorry for myself.

"What about the raccoons?" I ask.

"Do you want to invite them to perform?"

"Smart-ass. I mean, all the noise might freak 'em out?"

"Now you're grasping." Tabby leans forward, relieves me of my coffee cup, and grips my hands. "The show must go on, Hollie Porter. It's time for the Christmas Pageant Extravaganza."

We lock eyes for a few beats, and I know the battle is lost. "It's not a pageant. That makes it sound like we'll have scantily clad women sharing their views on world peace. Or worse, toddlers in evening gowns."

"OK, gross on that second visual, but considering how Mr. Richardson in room 34 found you last night, I'd say we could probably work in an act with a scantily clad woman, if you're up for it."

I yank my hands free and stand. "I hate you."

"You love me." Tabby stands and slides her phone into her back pocket. "Are you going to make the announcement, or shall I?"

"I should probably run it by Bill and Tanner first."

She flaps her hand at me. "They already said yes. You're the last blockade on the road to Pageant Town."

"It's a talent show."

Tabby whoops and pulls out her phone, hitting the preprogrammed number for who I assume is one among the proper management team. A male voice echoes through her speaker. "She said yes! We're on!"

She disconnects and throws an arm around my shoulders as we approach the doors that will release us back into the fray.

"Did you just call Bill? You should've let me talk to him about the raccoons."

As we exit the ballroom and round the bend to the concierge desk, a small crowd has gathered—Tanner, Bill, Cam, and Miss Betty—just outside the open doors to the storage room where our fuzzy, masked friends spent their evening. Acorn's inside, sniffing and snorting as if he were a bloodhound and not the Chef's overfed dog child.

"What ... is going on?"

"Good news!" Tanner says, the grin that reminds me so much of his brother puncturing his cheeks. "The raccoons are gone!"

"Oh. OK, that is good news. Um ... how? Where did they go?"

Tanner's glee melts like an icicle. Slowly, one muscle at a time until the worried grimace is back in place. "Well, that would be the bad news. We have no idea."

13

The whole vibe in the lodge changes once word gets out that Mean Hollie changed her mind about the talent show. As I have zero talents to share—unless people want a tutorial on CPR from my long-ago days as a 911 dispatcher—I will man the door and fetch drinks and snacks and smile with every "Hollie Berry" joke, *et cetera*. I've had my fill of dancing after last night's performance for Ryan (and an unwitting Mr. Richardson from room 34). And I'm pretty sure there's a law fresh from the provincial legislature down in Victoria that strictly prohibits me from singing anything other than the national anthem, and even then, I must be supervised.

With the storage closet vacated of last night's guests, Miss Betty was able to drag out her communication hub (a giant dry-erase board on wheels) so the show tunes nerds in residence could plan tonight's lineup. Guests are invited to participate if they have a bona fide talent. Last thing we need is a bunch of drunk hosers taking the stage to tell off-color jokes. No guarantees that won't happen among the staff who've already scribbled their names on Miss Betty's lobby playbill.

For now, I'm outside with Sarah, both of us bundled to the ears, shoveling snow off the pool tarp so it doesn't tear. We've already been down to the fake-ice rink to attempt to clean the fake ice of snow—a futile effort given the wind's refusal to menace someone else for a while. I think Bill reassigned us up here so we'd at least have the shadow of the lodge to protect us from the buffeting gusts. Bill's a nice guy. Like everyone's extra dad.

Although I don't need an extra dad because I have the best OG dad already. He called this morning to check in; they're encased in an ice storm down in Portland, so everything's jammed up there too. He filled me in on his big holiday plans—covering shifts at the hospital where he works as a nurse supervisor—and promised we would get together in the new year when everything thaws out. We talk at least once a week and throw memes at each other's phones on the daily, so Dad knows how much I miss him, how much I miss Ryan during hockey season. And he knows how much of a brat I can be when I don't get my own way.

On our call today, however, he was relieved to learn we're all safe and sound and warm, and he told me to toughen up and not make his awesome son-in-law feel bad about missing Christmas when "he's just out there earning an honest living like the rest of us."

That's my dad. Always the voice of reason. Except I threatened that if he decides he likes Ryan better than me, I will only invite Lucy Collins to use my friends-and-family discount. We had a good laugh because Lucy Collins can no longer darken my Canadian doorstep due to the wee little felonies attached to her passport.

Thank the Mounties.

"Hollie! I've got it!" Sarah pauses scooping, leaning on the handle of her shovel. She's not broken a sweat, whereas I am damp from head to toe, panting like I've run a marathon in weighted boots. Maybe if I were a cold-water, long-distance swimmer like my sister-in-law, I wouldn't look like the ill-formed, half-melted relative Frosty the Snowman doesn't like talking about. "You can dress up in the sea otter mascot costume and hang out with the kids for the talent show. Elsbeth would love that. We could even pin a Santa hat onto the head!"

"Fun idea, but the costume is on the mainland undergoing repairs." Couple years ago, we got a deal on a walk-around sea otter costume from the same company that made Fin, the Vancouver Canucks mascot. And then last summer, one of our guests helped himself to it, tried to wear it waterskiing, and screwed up the head. It's been at the mascot vet ever since, awaiting rescue by one of the Revelation Cove raft members.

"Oh, right. Damn it. That would've been fun." She resumes her work. The pool water under the tarp is not frozen solid, so we don't dare step on it, but Bill gave us this plastic rake thing with an extendable handle to scrape off layers to lighten the weight on the tarp. The snow's heavy, so it takes both of us to get a good pull, and even then, the pool deck is also buried in white, so there's nowhere to pile the scooped snow and yeah … it's a mess. While I'm a staunch feminist and stand in my luscious female power, yada yada yada, I'd really love it if a gallant dude with muscles and a hero complex would come outside and offer to finish this job for us so I could grab an Irish coffee and search the back office for my missing underwear.

An hour later, we declare the job "good enough" and trudge back indoors.

Miss Betty rushes at us down the hall, past the mini gallery of framed, signed hockey jerseys from a variety of NHL teams. She pauses before us, the sleeves on her Christmas cardigan pushed up to her elbows, her right hand fidgeting with the locket hanging around her neck.

"Mom?" Sarah asks. "Something wrong?"

"Have either of you seen Elsbeth?"

14

I t's not unusual for Elsbeth to play hide-and-seek in the lodge with her grownups, even when said grownups don't know the game is afoot. But Miss Betty works herself into a righteous froth, terrified the child has wandered down to the docks and fallen in. It's a legitimate fear when the ground is bare of snow, and Elsbeth has been told at least a thousand times to not go near the boats without her "life jackie" on.

I will not allow myself to worry more than is necessary, at least not yet. Especially since Miss Betty is practically hyperventilating. She was watching her granddaughter, who was happily sprawled on the back-office floor coloring in one of her activity books, and stepped out "just real quick to put together a snack for Els."

First thing, we check the walkways to and around the docks, looking for tiny footprints in the white powder, quickly realizing that the snow is so deep in spots, it would be practically impossible for Elsbeth to wade through it without getting stuck or giving up. And her little otter-print boots are still in the office—she's absolutely obsessed with them, as she is with most things I buy for her (which is a lot, yes, I know, I can't help that she's so cute, I'm compelled to reward her simply for being alive). We're confident she wouldn't go outside without her otter boots from Hollie Cat.

Since we don't want to panic anyone—we've already done enough to traumatize our guests in the last thirty-six hours—I post a gently worded but urgent inquiry on the resort group chat, just in case Elsbeth has decided to follow one of her new little friends when Miss Betty popped into the kitchen. Any staff who are not busy with guests are searching; Sarah runs to Miss Betty's apartment while Tanner checks all the potential hiding places in the main dining room and ballroom. I've checked the storage closet and back office twice, my pulse ratcheting up with every cupboard opened and every box moved that does not reveal the tiny form of my niece.

I move into the lobby, hands on hips as I turn slowly in a circle, trying to imagine where I would hide if I were five and full of mischief. According to my father, I *was* five and full of mischief at one point. "Elsbeth! Where are you hiding? Come on out so we can grab some of Gramma's Christmas cookies!"

Tabby opens the door to the spa and salon on the northernmost end of the lobby and shakes her head. "She's not in here either."

"Els, sweetie . . ." I move around the front desk to the sitting area with the plush couches, rich area rugs, and our giant Christmas tree. "Elsbeth, where are youuuuuu?" I sing.

"Do you think—"

I lift a hand to quiet Tabby. "Shh. Did you hear that?"

We freeze, ears perked.

A tiny giggle. It's close.

"Elllllsbeth . . ."

Another giggle. Tabby and I both spin toward the Christmas tree, and it's then I notice that one of the ginormous prop presents is tipped over near the back. I snap once at Tabby and point, mouthing *She's over there.*

Slowly, I tiptoe around the side of the tree, cooing my niece's name. "Princess Elsbie, have you escaped to your castle? Who will I share these delicious cookies with if I can't find you?"

"BOO!" Elsbeth jumps out from the red-wrapped appliance box.

Except she's not alone. In her arms is one of the raccoon kits, and behind her three more squeak and squeal as Momma Raccoon flies out of the tree at my head, hissing all the way.

15

Elsbeth, freshly bathed and in her tiny bathrobe after thorough inspection by both her mother and grandmother for ANY sign of broken skin, sobs in Sarah's arms about why she can't keep the baby raccoons. They tag-teamed and asked her a dozen times if any of the little critters had given her a bite or a nibble or a scrape or a kiss, and little Els cried and said, "No, they're my babies, they would never hurt me." We called the nurse helpline and then talked to a doctor at the ER in Nanaimo, and after two hours of consultation and another inspection of every inch of her extremities, it's decided we could wait for the winds to abate to take her in. We don't play the "fuck around and find out if you have rabies" game with raccoons.

Miss Betty tends to the impressive scrape on my face, earned when I tumbled into our plump Douglas fir to avoid the raccoon. The latest oozy insult to my person extends along my right cheek, eyebrow, and nearly into my hairline. After I came to live at Revelation Cove, Miss Betty took a bunch of first aid courses online and even did a week-long "citizen medic" workshop in Victoria, to become certified as our official Emergency First Responder. Given the amount of trouble I got myself into during my first year here, it seemed like the smart thing to do.

It's certainly come in handy today.

At first, they thought Momma Raccoon's claws or even teeth had carved the mark in my face. There was quite a bit of blood, as would be expected with an injury involving yours truly. However, I did not recall the furred outsider clutching my fleshy bits at any point, and upon closer inspection, including review of security footage, it was declared that I was, in fact, attacked by a rogue branch on the Christmas tree. How rude.

And yet I am grateful it didn't blind me, despite the unsavory gouge now decorating my otherwise unmarred complexion. Bummer thing is, my skin is only unmarred because I'm in that blissful week when my cycle-related acne takes a breather. (You'd think that by thirty, zits would be a thing of my distant past. *Au contraire!*) As Miss Betty inspects the damage and sets to cleaning my wound, she vacillates on whether we should head into Nanaimo immediately, just in case it was the raccoon. I reassure them I'm fine and remind her that until the wind calms its shit, we cannot go anywhere, and calling the Coast Guard for a scrape is probably not cool, given the likelihood they're dealing with *actual* emergencies.

"Maybe it's a good thing Ryan won't be home tonight. Who wants to look at *this*?" I joke, sucking air through my teeth as Miss Betty presses the ointment-covered Q-Tip too deep.

I'm seated at the breakfast bar in my mother-in-law's kitchen, her industrial-grade first aid kit sprawled open on the countertop. My ringtone interrupts the quiet, earning me a side-eye from Sarah —Elsbeth was almost asleep in her mother's arms, but Els knows Ryan's ringtone, so her head pops off Sarah's shoulder. "Unca! Unca! I wanna talk to him!"

"Sorry," I whisper, then hop off the barstool and move toward the bathroom to answer.

"She's awake now. Just answer it so she can talk to him," Sarah says, sighing as she plops onto the couch and releases her squirming daughter.

"Hey, Ry," I answer.

51

"Porter, seriously? Is everyone OK?"

"Everyone's fine. Elsbeth is completely unharmed, other than a broken heart that she can't keep her baby bandits. And your mom is tending my wound—"

"Wait—you're wounded? Tanner didn't mention a wound."

"I scratched my face on the Christmas tree."

"Are you sure it wasn't from the mother raccoon? Hols, you know we do not mess around with rabies."

"Babe, I know. It's not from the raccoon. I kinda fell into the tree when the momma launched—you know what, it's fine. I'm *fine*. Your mom is fixing things, and we'll go to Nanaimo as soon as we're not at risk of checking in to Davy Jones' locker should we embark upon an aquatic voyage." I'm trying to speak in euphemisms so Elsbeth doesn't pick up any unnecessary fear about going in the boat.

Ryan responds, but I can't hear him because Elsbeth is losing her ever-loving mind about talking to her favorite uncle. "Ryan, gonna ask you to pause whatever you're saying and talk to Els first before her head explodes."

I hand the phone to my niece who puts it to her ear and then tucks her shoulder close to hold it. She's a pro. At five. And with her tiny rainbow-painted fingernails and the terry-cloth robe, her little mouth chattering as fast as she can form words to regale Unca with how mean we all are for not letting her keep the "rancoons," my mind does that fast-forward glimpse thing where I see her as a teenager, phone propped against her head as she unloads about whatever recent injustice she has suffered at the hands of her very uncool family.

"Unca, why can't you come home for Christmas? We have lots of snow and we can make a snow family and Gramma made SO much cookies. Can't you just fly your plane? The water doesn't have snow on it, so why can't you land Miss Lily like you always do?"

Ryan's voice buzzes low through the phone's speaker as he talks to his niece, and it dawns on me as I watch her that she looks so much like her dad . . . which means she looks so much like Ryan.

Maybe what our baby girl would look like.

Uh, what the hell, Hollie . . . Where did that come from?

"OK, bye, Unca. I asked Santa to bring you home for Christmas, so I'll see you soon!"

She drops the phone on the couch and launches into a solo performance of original choreography that mostly involves hopping and spinning and singing at the top of her lungs.

I scoop up my cell. "Whatever you said, she's dancing now. Thank you."

"I *am* her favorite."

"You're her favorite *uncle*. I'm her favorite Hollie Cat." I lift a finger to indicate a pause and wander into Miss Betty's bedroom for a moment's quiet. The view from this window is never not impressive, but right now, with the blanket of white covering everything and the sky purpling toward dusk, I again whisper a quiet thanks to whatever deities conspired to plant me here.

"How are things on your side of the strait?" I ask. "How are the roads?"

"Dumb. And the winds are picking up. Power's out in White Rock, Richmond, and parts of Surrey."

"Shit."

"The lights have flickered a few times. Worst-case scenario, the five boys here will head over to Nils's place. He has a generator. And his mom and sisters are in town, so they're better equipped to feed a hockey team than I am at the moment."

"Right." Nils has a house. A nice house with acreage and lots of space. Ryan and I have talked about houses, but the market is utter madness and we can't justify a mortgage if it's just him living on the mainland, especially since the hockey club covers half the rent on the Langley apartment *and* we live basically for free at the Cove.

"I'm sorry, Hollie. I know you're upset."

"It is what it is," I say, trying to hide the emotion burning my throat. "We'll see each other in a couple days. This shit can't last forever."

"You didn't just say that out loud, did you?"

I chuckle to hide my sniff. "Did Tanner tell you the talent show is back on?"

"He did."

"It's like herding cats in this place sometimes."

"You mean all the time?"

The line is quiet, and I know I need to hang up before I start bawling. "Um, I gotta go so I can get a Band-Aid. I love you. Call me with any updates."

"I love you too, Hols. So much."

"'K, bye." I hit the red button, pluck a Kleenex from the box on Miss Betty's dresser, and wince as the first salty tear rolls into the raw, open wound on my cheek.

16

The talent show is as chaotic as I expected it to be. I had my jokes at the ready about how loosely we use the term "talent," but I was pleasantly surprised. So many of our staff can sing, play, dance, do magic tricks, and tell way better jokes than I could ever come up with. And among the guests, we have two *very* accomplished pianists who wowed us with Christmas songs; one of our regulars, a lawyer in real life, has a voice like velvet and showcased his talents with multiple selections from the rather un-Christmassy *Les Misérables*; a Vancouver Symphony Orchestra violinist had her instrument with her, so she played a piece from *The Nutcracker*; and her wife, a soprano with the Vancouver Opera, jumped up to duet with the singing lawyer on a *Les Mis* song that choked up the whole room.

I had *no idea* I was surrounded by such talent.

Consider me schooled.

The talent show I thought would be a total waste of resources turns out to be exactly what we all need. While we still don't have electricity, the generators are cooperating in their task of providing lights and heat, the fireplaces are continuously monitored, fed, and stoked, our creative bartenders have outdone themselves with clever

Christmas cocktails, and Chef has set up a charcuterie buffet for the ages.

As the last performers take their bows—Brad and his not-terrible band who call themselves the Garden Gnomes—one of the pianists resumes her seat behind the baby grand and begins a rousing rendition of "Santa Claus Is Coming to Town" while the singers gather onstage and invite everyone to join in. As bummed as I've been with the storm stress, last night's *very* embarrassing cybercoitus interruptus, Raccoonageddon, and the reality that my fifth Christmas as a married woman will be without the other half of my heart, even I am not immune to the infectious spirit overtaking the ballroom. Sarah and Tanner and I trade off dancing with Elsbeth who sings at the top of her lungs, making up the words as she goes along.

The song reaches its crescendo, and from behind the makeshift curtain prances Santa Claus—Bill in an amply padded Santa costume and long white beard, accompanied by Acorn outfitted in his own festive red suit and an impressive set of antlers. Santa waves at the kids, ho-ho-ho'ing above their excited shrieks, a bulky sack thrown over his shoulder. Acorn barks his seasons' greetings, although I'd guess he's probably yelling in dog language that it's really damn loud in here and can everyone just take it down a notch, *thanks very much.*

With the singing concluded, the pianist continues with a quiet serenade as Santa seats himself on an overstuffed chair and calls up the kids one by one to receive whatever presents their parents secretly stashed within his burgeoning bag of joy. When Santa calls Elsbeth's name, she sprints forward and then stops to straighten her Christmas dress before taking the two small steps up with all the grace of a princess. You can tell we're not related by blood—she doesn't trip and break her nose while collecting her present from the giant red elf. And when she steps close and throws her arms around Bill's—I mean, Santa's—neck, a collective "Awww!" echoes through the room, punctuated by the blinding flash of Miss Betty's camera.

After presents have been distributed, Santa stands, offers warm Christmas wishes, and tells all the kids he has to get back to his sleigh so he can visit the rest of the world before the sun comes up. Everyone waves him offstage, and the pianist wraps up with "We Wish You a Merry Christmas" as guests gather their things and their children. Thanks and hugs are exchanged, and more than a few revelers are a little wobblier on their feet than they were at the outset of our Christmas Pageant Extravaganza.

Pageant. Talent show. Whatever.

The fun's not over, though, as much as I'd like to go back to my cold, lonely bed and uncork a bottle of Prosecco and pop in the Blu-Ray of *It's a Wonderful Life*. No, ladies and germs, we still have the Revelation Cove Staff portion of this evening's fete. I fear that means more noise from the Garden Gnomes, so in preparation, I step behind the bar cart and help myself to an unopened sparkling wine. It's warm, but I'm not a fancy girl. Plus, maybe the 12.5% ABV will make me forget how much my serrated face stings.

Brad and two of his guys move one of the festive round tables onto the stage where Tabby and her salon assistant, both dressed as sexy elves, make quick work of unloading two totes of Secret Santa presents. Brad then sets up his iPhone in a dock and blasts hard rock, but only until Miss Betty points at him and shakes her head. Anyone who's lived and worked at Revelation Cove for more than a couple hours knows that look. He rolls his eyes and grabs his phone to find a playlist more suited to the occasion.

As Bing Crosby croons the first notes of "I'm Dreaming of a White Christmas," Miss Betty's eyes widen and sparkle, her hand flattened over her heart. Yeah, Brad's got the boss's number.

With the guests cleared out, we've all gathered around the front near the stage, each person waiting until their name is called to collect their gift and then we'll all open them together. Some debate circulated in the group chat about whether we should play Vicious Christmas, but thankfully, the idea was vetoed by a wide margin. People wanted to get real presents for the coworker whose name they drew, not throwaway garbage or jokey stuff that could be plucked or traded. And since people are already three sheets to the wind, the last thing we need is a barroom brawl over the most prized gift in the room.

"Hey, Hols, do you want a glass for that?" Tanner asks, nodding at the bottle clutched in my fist.

"Nah. I'm good." I take a long swig. He shakes his head at me and laughs.

"Hollie knows how to handle her liquor," Sarah says from my other side. I lift my hand for a high five. Elsbeth, sitting at the table just behind us, runs a comb through the pink and purple plastic hair of the My Little Pony she just opened from Santa Bill. She's again singing an original Christmas composition, lost in her own world. This kid, man—she's absolutely wrapped in family who loves her. She will never want for anything, never wonder if her mom loves her or know the hollow pain of thinking herself not good enough, not worthy of her mother's love.

Shit. I lift the wine bottle in front of me. How much have I drunk already?

"OK, that's the last one!" Tabby hollers, tossing a wrapped present toward Tanner and nodding at me. He hands it over. I look down at the tag—*To Hollie, from Your Secret Santa*—the scrawl nearly illegible. "One, two, three! Everyone open!"

The room fills with the sound of ripping and tearing, followed quickly by laughs, hollers, and hoots. I slide into a chair adjacent to my niece and set my wine down long enough to open my present.

"Whaddya get, Hollie Cat?" Elsbeth peeks over her pony.

I laugh. It's a three-pack of Band-Aids printed with sea otters. I hold them up so Els can see.

"Hey, you can use those on your face right now! Do you want me to help you?" She drops her plastic comb and jumps out of her chair, eager to play doctor.

"Thank you! Whoever these are from!" I announce, lifting the box over my head before Elsbeth tears into it and slathers me in adhesive strips.

The music cuts out midsong, eliciting groans that maybe the power is failing again—but then the room fills with a new tune, this one very much not a Christmas jingle.

A slow guitar lead-in. Sultry, haunting, but sensuous. I recognize that riff.

Because I played it last night.

The crowd silences, and stage left, a giant sea otter in an ugly Christmas sweater slinks and shimmies from behind the curtain.

I mean, it's not a *real* sea otter but rather someone dressed in a sea otter costume. *Our* sea otter costume. The one that's been at the mascot vet for months.

When Chris Isaak's voice slides through the speakers, the sea otter gyrates, turns, and wiggles its butt, then spins back around. My work family is no longer docile but raising the roof with their catcalls and whoops.

I don't dare get my hopes up . . .

Then the sea otter pulls something from the pocket of the Christmas sweater, slowly, teasing it free. Pinched in its fingers, the otter spins it above its head, thick midsection rotating in what I think is supposed to be an Elvis-inspired hip thrust.

And then it hits me: THOSE ARE MY PANTIES.

From last night.

If I weren't cackling to the point of breathlessness, I'd be mortified.

The otter slows its awkward mating dance and shuffles to the stage edge, right arm outstretched with furred paw pointing straight ahead, its left hand still twirling the panties like the starting flag at a NASCAR race. The crowd parts as the otter hops down—

And drops onto its knees right in front of me.

Everyone erupts into applause as I lift the sea otter's huge head from its shoulders.

And underneath is the world's most beautiful, wonderful, adorable Ryan Fielding, grinning at me with that look that says he knows he's a man who is getting laid tonight.

"Hi," I say, his cheeks cupped in my shaking hands. Fresh tears sting my owie, but I've never been happier for pain.

"Hi yourself," he says. "I think these are yours." My panties hang from his outstretched finger.

I snag them, stuff 'em in my pocket, and throw myself onto my human sea otter for a not-safe-for-work kiss.

17

I wait long enough for Ryan to greet and hug his mother, brother, and sister-in-law, and of course, Elsbeth who jumped up onto one of the banquet tables to announce, "See, Hollie Cat? I TOLD you Santa would bring Unca home for Christmas!" Ryan circulates for handshakes and half hugs, and when Bill tries to loop him into a conversation about the generators and how we will probably be out of fuel by morning, I intervene, emboldened by the twenty or so ounces of Prosecco sloshing around in my gut.

"No. It is Christmas. My husband will be available to talk about biomass bullshit in the morning. GOOD NIGHT, EVERYONE!" I grab Ryan's right arm with both hands and pull, walking backward as I tow him from the ballroom still in the otter costume (sans head) as he waves to his adoring crowd. Once we're in the lobby, he scoops me into a bridal carry and runs down the hall toward the residence wing, practically bouncing me out of his grasp more than once. I hold tight, squealing the whole way, not even caring if I wake the entire island.

Ryan stops in front of our door, releasing me only long enough so I can dig out my key card from my borrowed, sequined clutch.

He again lifts me off my feet and glides over the threshold into our love nest, but instead of hightailing it to the bedroom as I'd hoped, he slides me onto the kitchen island. The marble is cold under my ass—I'm dressed in tights and the closest thing I have to Christmas attire, some green and black plaid minidress Sarah dug out of the back of her closet.

Ryan turns around so I can reach under the hideously awesome Christmas sweater and unzip the otter costume. He shimmies free as it puddles on the floor and faces me again.

"You're wearing a tuxedo?" I ask.

He smiles like a cat who just swallowed an entire pet store of canaries. "I wanted to look pretty for you." He then moves between my knees, his warm hands sliding up my thighs, under the hem of the dress, until he reaches the crease where my legs join my torso. I shiver from head to toe.

"And the otter costume is fixed." I nod at the furry pile.

"Indeed. We will be keeping that locked in a safe." We share a quiet laugh.

Ryan then extracts his left hand to tip my chin slightly. Without touching, he inspects the Tannenbaum's terror stretched along my right cheek. He smirks, shakes his head, and tucks my hair behind my ear.

"Am I too scary to look at?" I ask.

"Never." His left hand journeys under my skirt again, this time heading right for the honey as his lips meet mine. "Goddamn, I've missed you, woman."

Grateful the tree didn't scrape holes in the parts of my face I use to kiss and lick my husband, I wholeheartedly follow Ryan's lead in the tongue tango I've been dreaming about for weeks.

He leans back, his breath sweet and hot on my face. "I have it on good authority that you have been a *very* naughty girl this year." He reaches back and pulls the clip from my hair, releasing the dirty-blond waves around my shoulders.

"Pretty naughty. But not nearly as naughty as I'm going to be once I extract my sex machine from his tuxedo." I reach between us and flatten a hand over his crotch. Yeah, the sex machine is definitely fueled and ready to go.

No generator needed.

18

"Porter . . . wake up." Warm, full lips kiss my neck, across my collarbone, down my boob. A tongue flicks my nipple.

"Keep doing that and I'll wake up."

He leans over and administers the same care to my other boob. "It's snowing again," he whispers between licks.

I crack my eyelids and look toward our huge window. A gap in the curtains indeed reveals chonky white flakes drifting slowly earthward, the atmospheric backdrop a muted midnight gray. "What time is it?"

"Just after two." Ryan ceases the careful lavage of my nipples to slide from the bed and throw apart the curtains. He stands with hands on hips looking over his domain, silhouetted against the falling snow, his thirty-six-year-old body still a work of muscled art. Evidence of our run-in with Chloe the Cougar a few years ago is still prevalent, but between reconstructive surgeries and countless hours of top-notch physiotherapy, he's recovered about eighty percent strength on that side.

"Come back to bed. I require affection."

He turns wearing a wide grin, my favorite grin, his teeth practically glowing in the ambient light spill. "*More* affection?"

"Yes, Coach. All the affection."

He slides under the covers and pulls me against his chest, tugging to make sure I'm covered with the blankets. He buries his face in my hair and inhales. "Thank you for dealing with everything. I'm sorry I wasn't here."

"It's fine. We have an awesome team. We handled it."

"I knew you would. You always do." He kisses the side of my head. "The storm and power outage, the guy from room 34 walking in on us last night, the raccoons today . . . you know what that is, don't you?"

"Another day in the life of Hollie Porter Fielding?"

He snickers. "That, my dear, is a hat trick."

Three goals, one game. A hat trick. He's right. "Except I think more than just three things went wrong."

"Still, you handled it. I am so proud of you, babe."

"Thanks . . . and I'm so happy and proud of *you* for finding a way home to me."

"Yeah, not gonna lie. The boat ride here was scary as fuck."

"You're an idiot," I say, pinching his side under the covers. He jerks and laughs.

"The winds had died down enough on the mainland that the ferries were running again. I wouldn't have tried it otherwise."

"You couldn't fly?"

"Miss Lily is in Victoria, and I didn't want to waste the window of calm by stopping there first, fueling up, all that."

"Right. Wait—" I lean up on my left elbow. His eyes sparkle in the dim light. "Whose boat did you use?"

"Nils'."

"Doesn't Nils have a *speedboat*?"

Ryan shrugs and pulls me back down to him. "I made it just fine. At least I didn't take a rowboat out in a thunderstorm to commune with orca like *some* people I know."

I pinch him again. He yelps and flips me onto my back, my wrists pinned above my head on the pillow as he eases his body between my legs. Again. "What did I tell you about pinching?" He crushes his lips to mine and grinds into my pelvis before pulling back.

"Tease."

He snorts. "I am anything but a tease." He releases my wrists and leans on his left arm so his weight is mostly off me, our bodies still touching. I drape my left leg over his hip in encouragement. "Hols, maybe I should hang up my skates. Come home. I can't stand being away from you so much."

"Ryan, no. Babe, seriously?" I flatten a hand against his cheek. His beard is so soft. "If you quit coaching, you'll regret it. You are giddy when you're behind that bench. And those kids *need* you."

He pulls my wrist from his face and cradles my hand in his much bigger one. His thumb caresses the bracelet I haven't taken off since the day he gave it to me at the Vancouver Aquarium after I pulled a runner, days before our wedding.

"Our raft, our rules." He whispers the words engraved on the silver surface. He lifts my hand to his mouth and kisses my palm. "I would do anything to make you happy, Hollie. And I know how miserable I've been over in Langley without you. Yeah, I'm fine on the ice, but when I get home and it's so quiet and our bed is cold and lonely . . . I don't want to be one of those husbands who makes his wife mold her entire life around his career."

I laugh and look at the beautiful room around us. "Yeah, 'cuz it's been a real hardship so far, let me tell you."

He intertwines our fingers. "You know what I mean."

"Rafts float together. I float where you float and vice versa. Watching you coach is basically the wind beneath my wings, so you're not giving that up."

He leans close and gently nips my lower lip with his teeth. I pull my hand free and lace it through his dark waves, deepening the kiss. Ryan moves over me again, preparing to prove he's not a tease.

"Ryan . . ." I mumble against his lips.

He unseals his mouth from mine for a beat, our eyes locked in the sensuous dark.

"What about if I come ashore for a while . . ."

His eyes widen and he eases back, adjusting his weight ever so slightly. "What do you mean?"

"I mean . . . I can do my job from anywhere. Maybe we should pick up that conversation about, you know, a house. Maybe a house with a couple extra bedrooms, just in case."

"Hollie . . ." My name floats on his breath. "Are you serious?"

I move my hips just so, lining up his stick with the mouth of the goal. "What is that you mentioned about a hat trick?"

Ryan's eyes glisten with what I suspect is emotion, his smile so wide I'm afraid he'll pull a muscle as he drives himself home. "Porter, you know I always shoot to score."

Join the Raft!

If you want to be among the first to hear about new and upcoming Eliza Gordon books, audiobooks, and projects, join the Raft!

Join my private readers' group on Facebook, or sign up for my newsletter! Welcome aboard!

(P.S. Otter illustration above by Heather at Illustrate-it.ca. Check her out!)

In the wild, sea otters hold hands so they aren't separated in the tides. These groups of floating otters are called "rafts."

About the Author

A native of Portland, Oregon, Eliza Gordon (a.k.a. Jennifer Sommersby) has always lived along the West Coast. Since 2002, home has been a suburb of Vancouver, British Columbia. When not lost in a writing project, she works as a freelance editor (via Plumfield Editing), mom, wife, bibliophile, Superman freak, and humble servant to three pampered tuxedo cats (@tuxietrionurojo on Instagram).

Eliza writes women's fiction, romantic comedy, and enviromance; Jennifer Sommersby writes young adult fiction. Both personalities are represented by Stacey Kondla at The Rights Factory.

Want to buy direct from Eliza? Visit the SGA Books Shopify store!

Find the Eliza Gordon books at the following retailers in e-book, print, and audio.

Did you know you can ask your local library to order in Eliza's books?

Visit elizagordon.com for links.

SGA
BOOKS

www.ingramcontent.com/pod-product-compliance
Lightning Source LLC
Chambersburg PA
CBHW030510130626
46549CB00007B/2924